The Princess
and the
Porcupines

A humorous
fantasy story

First published in 2005 by
Franklin Watts
96 Leonard Street
London
EC2A 4XD

Franklin Watts Australia
Level 17/207 Kent Street
Sydney
NSW 2000

A CIP catalogue record for this book is available
from the British Library.

ISBN 0 7496 6138 0 (hbk)
ISBN 0 7496 6144 5 (pbk)

Series Editor: Jackie Hamley
Series Advisors: Dr Barrie Wade, Dr Hilary Minns
Design: Peter Scoulding

Printed in China

The Princess
and the
Porcupines

Written by
Damian Harvey

Illustrated by
Andy Catling

W
FRANKLIN WATTS
LONDON•SYDNEY

Damian Harvey
"The idea for this story came after seeing a circus where a man, dressed like a prince, lay on a very spiky bed... Ouch!"

Andy Catling
"I like porcupines. They like to dance, sing and pull silly faces. But I never hug them too tight, because they're prickly in places!"

Princess Petunia lived in a grand palace with the King and Queen.

The King and Queen wanted Petunia
to have the best of everything.

She had the finest clothes ...

... the most dazzling jewels ...

... and the prettiest ponies.

7

When the time came for Petunia to marry, the King and Queen wanted her to have the perfect Prince for a husband.

8

Princes came from near and far
to prove they were good enough
to marry the Princess.

But the King and Queen didn't
think any one of them was fit
for their daughter.

Petunia thought she'd never find
a Prince good enough for the King
and Queen.

Until, that is, Prince Aldini came
to call at the palace.

Prince Aldini charmed the King ...

... and swept the Queen off her feet.

"He's perfect!" said Princess Petunia.

But the King and Queen still weren't sure.

So they tried to think of the hardest

test that they could for Prince Aldini.

Finally, they decided. "Only the bravest, most perfect of princes could sleep soundly on a bed of porcupines!" said the Queen.

Princess Petunia was sure that Prince
Aldini would fail the test.

The King and Queen were sure, too.

Prince Aldini slept soundly all night.
The King and Queen were amazed.

But they had to keep their promise.

So Prince Aldini and Princess Petunia
were married.

They had a grand wedding and lived

happily ever after ...

... for most of the time!

Notes for parents and teachers

READING CORNER has been structured to provide maximum support for new readers. The stories may be used by adults for sharing with young children. Primarily, however, the stories are designed for newly independent readers, whether they are reading these books in bed at night, or in the reading corner at school or in the library.

Starting to read alone can be a daunting prospect. **READING CORNER** helps by providing visual support and repeating words and phrases, while making reading enjoyable. These books will develop confidence in the new reader, and encourage a love of reading that will last a lifetime!

If you are reading this book with a child, here are a few tips:

1. Make reading fun! Choose a time to read when you and the child are relaxed and have time to share the story.

2. Encourage children to reread the story, and to retell the story in their own words, using the illustrations to remind them what has happened.

3. Give praise! Remember that small mistakes need not always be corrected.

READING CORNER covers three grades of early reading ability, with three levels at each grade. Each level has a certain number of words per story, indicated by the number of bars on the spine of the book, to allow you to choose the right book for a young reader:

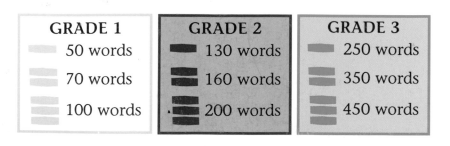

GRADE 1	GRADE 2	GRADE 3
50 words	130 words	250 words
70 words	160 words	350 words
100 words	200 words	450 words